Come On, Danny

by

Andy Croft

Illustrated by Julia Page

First published in 2009 in Great Britain by
Barrington Stoke Ltd
18 Walker St, Edinburgh, EH3 7LP

www.barringtonstoke.co.uk

ISBN: 978-1-84299-616-4

Printed in Great Britain by Bell & Bain Ltd

A Note from the Author

I've spent a lot of time in prison. Working. Over the years I have worked with hundreds of prisoners. Helping them to write stories and poems about their lives.

I enjoy working in prisons. But they can be sad places. Prisoners are full of regrets. Some wish they had worked harder at school. Many wish they had never started using drugs. All of them wish they could see more of their children.

Everyone wants to be a good dad. But how can you be when you are banged up? A visit can keep prisoners cheerful for days. But it can also remind them what they are missing. I've seen children crying when their dad has to go back to his cell. And I've seen men in tears after a visit from their children.

This book is for them.

Contents

Chapter 1

Not Again

"Not again!"

Danny pulled his football kit out of the bag. It was still damp and muddy. He hated playing in wet kit. The Year 8s were playing Benton after school. Benton had beaten them twice last season. Danny wanted to win this one.

There was no time for breakfast. Anyway, there was no food in the kitchen. Just a lot of empty bottles and cans. His older brother, Mark, was in last night with his mates. Danny would get some crisps at the shops.

There was no sign of his mum. She must be still in bed. Danny stuffed his muddy kit into a plastic bag. He let himself out. It was raining. It always seemed to be raining.

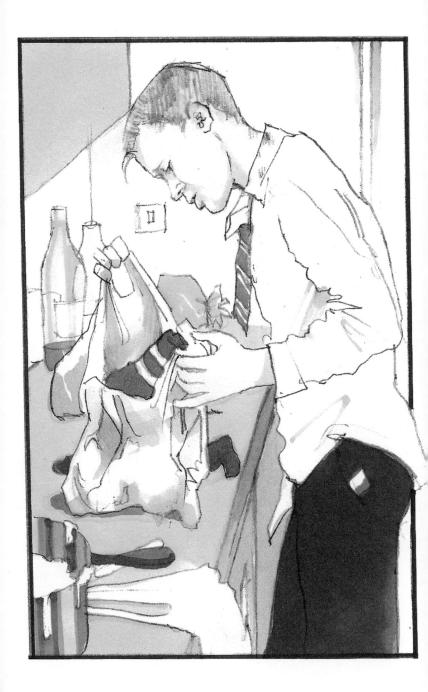

Baz and Lee were waiting for him outside the shops.

"You done that maths?" asked Danny.

"Yeah, right!" said Baz.

Lee looked at Danny as if he was crazy. "God, I hate school," he said.

"Only three more years ..." said Baz.

Baz and Lee hated school, because they always did badly. All Danny's mates hated it. At least they said they did. For some reason they wanted Danny to hate it too. But Danny liked school. He always had. Sometimes he pretended he didn't like it. Just so the others wouldn't call him a teacher's pet.

Danny liked English best. He liked reading. And he liked writing stories. He wrote about all kinds of things. Being a hero. Being grown up. Being happy. Seeing his dad again. Anything could happen in a story. You just made things up. It was like making a wish ...

Chapter 2

Fishing

Danny didn't remember much about his dad. Just the dark blue tattoos all over his arms and neck. Snakes and daggers and spider's webs. If he shaved his head there was a huge dragon on his skull. When Danny was small he was scared of the dragon.

His mum and dad split up when Danny was a baby. But his dad used to come round and take Danny out. Most of the time they just kicked a ball on the field behind their house.

One time his dad threw a rope over the branch of a tree. Danny was scared to swing out over the little stream. Then his dad showed him how to hold on. It was brilliant. Danny felt like he was flying. Soon all the other kids wanted a go. Danny was so proud of his dad that day.

Another time his dad took him fishing. Someone lent them a van and they drove out to some woods near the sea. In the middle of the woods was a pond. It was dead quiet. They were the only people there. Like it was a secret place. Their secret place.

They stayed there all afternoon, waiting for the fish to bite. Danny ate some crisps while his dad smoked. They could hear a cuckoo calling in the woods. His dad told him the names of the birds and the trees. It was very hot. Time seemed to slow down. Danny watched the sun-light dance on the water. He wanted the afternoon to last for ever.

They didn't catch anything that day. But it didn't matter. On the way home they stopped for fish and chips. "The only fish we're going to see today," joked his dad.

A few weeks later his dad was banged up. Danny wanted to visit him in prison. But his mum wouldn't take him. Said she was too busy. Then they moved his dad to another prison. Somewhere down South. Danny didn't even know the address. That was over seven years ago.

Chapter 3

Boffin

English was last lesson. Mrs Wilson was Danny's favourite teacher. She was also Danny's form tutor. He loved the way she used words. Interesting words. Good words. She said she liked the stories he made up. She sometimes gave him books to read at home.

This term they were writing pretend life-stories. Mrs Wilson asked them what they wanted to do when they left school. All the boys said they wanted to be footballers. Most of the girls wanted to be models. Baz said he was going to be a speed-way rider. Lee said he was going to be a porn star. Everyone laughed.

"And what about you, Danny?" said Mrs Wilson.

They all turned to look at him.

"He's going to be a mad scientist, Miss," said Lee.

Everyone laughed.

"Boffin! Boffin!"

"Stop that now," said Mrs Wilson. "Well, Danny?"

Danny didn't know what to say. He wanted to be a teacher. Like Mrs Wilson. But he couldn't say it. The other kids would laugh.

"He's going to be locked up, Miss. Like his dad," said one girl.

Everyone laughed again.

"Or a prossie like his mum," said another.

"Stop that now," said Mrs Wilson, getting cross. "Come on, Danny, what do you want to be?"

Danny took a deep breath.

"I just want to be a footballer, Miss," he said.

Chapter 4

Hungry

The Year 8 team were winning 2–0.

"Come on, Danny!" Mrs Wilson shouted.

Danny looked up and smiled. He megged a defender and crossed the ball. Baz headed it in. Yes! 3–0.

Danny was good. Even Mrs Wilson could see that. Perhaps he would make it one day. But she didn't think so. Only the very best made it to the top. And Danny wasn't *that* good. Anyway, Danny was different. He could do something else. If he wanted to.

Danny was running down the wing. He dummied one defender. Then the next. Only the keeper to beat. Yes! 4–0.

By the time Danny got home he was hungry. He looked in the kitchen for food. Just some tea-bags, sliced bread and some eggs. Not even any milk. The bread was hard. As usual.

Danny opened the living-room door. His older brother, Mark, was in there with his mates. The blinds were down. The TV was on. Some stupid cartoon. The room stank of dope.

"We won," said Danny.

No answer.

"Where's Mum?"

Still no answer.

"Mark – has Mum left any money for my tea?"

No answer.

Danny slammed the door and went up to his room. He looked in his pockets. Not even any money for some crisps.

He got his homework out on the floor. At the top of the page he wrote "My Life as a Footballer". Then he put his pen down.

Someone put on some loud music in the living-room. The floor started to shake. Danny sat on the edge of his bed and stared out of the window. Some kids were trying to start a fire in the middle of the road. It was raining again.

Chapter 5

Bad News

Danny didn't believe it. Mrs Wilson was standing at the front of the class.

"As some of you may know," she said, "I am leaving to have a baby."

Some of the kids giggled.

"Mr Harris, the head-teacher, will teach you English until the end of term."

Danny groaned. Old Harris had never liked him. He didn't know why. Harris seemed to pick on him.

Mrs Wilson asked Danny to stay behind at the end of the lesson. He still hadn't written anything about his life as a footballer.

"It's not like you, Danny," she said.

"I'm sorry, Miss," he said, "it's just –"

"What, Danny?"

"Nothing, Miss," he said.

"Any problems at home?"

If only she knew. But Danny didn't know where to start.

"No, Miss. I'll finish the story tonight."

When he got home his mum was watching TV. There was a man sitting next to her. He had one arm round her. And a can of beer in the other.

"Oh, it's you," said his mum. "This is Terry. You'll be seeing a lot of each other." Danny's mum lit another fag. "So you'd better get used to it."

The thin man grinned at Danny. His two front teeth were missing. He stank of beer and fags.

This boy-friend looked worse than the last one. If that was possible. The last one used to pinch money from Danny's mum's bag. He once slapped Danny. Just because Danny wouldn't lend him a fiver.

"Whatever." Danny shrugged and slammed out of the house. It was still raining.

Chapter 6

Nice One

Baz and Lee were sitting on the roof of the bus-stop. Baz was holding a big bottle of cider.

"Coming down the field?"

"I can't," said Danny. He had to finish his English course-work. But then he remembered. Mrs Wilson was leaving. Old Harris already hated him. What was the point? Why not go with them?

"OK," he sighed.

Baz and Lee jumped down, laughing.

Some other kids were already there. One of them was on the swing. Some were passing round a joint. Baz necked the last of the cider and threw the bottle into the

stream. Someone was trying to set fire to a chair with lighter-fuel.

"It's the Nutty Professor!" someone yelled. "Done your homework?"

Everyone laughed. Danny went red. He sat down on the wet grass. One of the girls offered Danny the joint. Danny shook his head.

"He's got to keep his brain cells clean," said Lee, "for Mrs Wilson."

"Fancy her, do you?"

"Of course not," said Danny.

"But she fancies him," said Baz. "Proper teacher's pet, aren't you, Danny?"

Danny didn't say anything. It would only make things worse. He made up his mind to go home. Just then one of the younger kids ran over.

"Look what I've found!" he yelled.

They all gathered round. A small lump of spiky fur lay curled up on the grass. One of the girls poked it with a stick.

"What is it?"

"A hedgehog."

"What are we going to do with it?"

"Kill it!"

"Let's set fire to it!"

Baz grabbed the lighter fuel. He poured some on the little hedgehog. One of the girls had some matches.

"Stop!" Danny yelled.

They all turned to look at him.

"Got a better plan, Mr Brain-box? Or are you scared?"

Danny thought fast. He picked up the hedgehog and threw it up in the air. It

landed in the stream with a splash. The other kids stared at him. Then they cheered.

"Nice one, Danny," said Lee, "nice one."

They turned to go. Danny looked back. Something crawled out of the water and into the bushes. Danny smiled to himself. He had read somewhere that hedgehogs could swim.

Chapter 7

Not Fair

"So you thought it was clever did you?"

"No, Miss."

Things were looking bad for Danny.
Someone had told the RSPCA about the
hedgehog. The RSPCA had told the police.

The police had rung the school. The head-teacher had spoken to Mrs Wilson. And now she was speaking to him. In front of the whole class.

Her face was white with anger. He had never seen her so cross.

"How could you be so cruel?" She was shouting now. "Drowning a hedgehog!"

"But, Miss –"

"I'm not interested in your excuses, Danny."

"But, Miss, I was only –"

"You were what? Only having a laugh? Well, I don't think it's very funny."

"No, Miss."

Mrs Wilson shook her head. "I just don't understand you, Danny. I thought you were different. But you're just as stupid as the rest." She glared round the classroom.

"Yes, Miss."

"Mr Harris wants to see you in his office."

"Yes, Miss."

"Now!"

Danny was excluded from school for the rest of the week. The police came round to talk to his mum. Afterwards she yelled at him. So did her boy-friend. It wasn't fair.

Over the next few weeks Danny started missing lessons. And English most of all. He couldn't be bothered to finish his English course-work. Then he started missing school.

He hated school now. Just like Baz and Lee and the rest. He hated Mr Harris. He hated Mrs Wilson. He hated his mum. He hated his life. Perhaps Mark and his druggie mates were right. Everything was rubbish.

Danny was on his own now.

Chapter 8

Penalty!

The Year 8 team were playing in the quarter-final. Against Parkway. Danny's football kit was still wet and muddy. But he wasn't playing. He was sub. They were already losing 1–0. It looked like Parkway would walk it.

Then Lee scored a lucky goal in the second half. With five minutes to go Baz was tripped in the box. Penalty! Danny always took the penalties. Baz was hurt. The PE teacher told Danny to go on for Baz.

Danny placed the ball on the spot and stepped back. He tried to clear his mind. To focus. The crowd was cheering. Then he heard what they were saying. They were chanting, "Hedgehog! Hedgehog! Hedgehog! Hedgehog!"

That was it. Danny didn't care any more.
He hated everyone and everything. He would
show them. He was going to miss. He
wouldn't even try. That would show them.
All of them. He stepped up to shoot.

Then he heard a voice he had not heard
for a long time. "Come on, Danny! Come on,
Danny!"

He looked up. There was a blur of blue
tattoo behind the goal.

Danny swung his left foot as hard as he could. The ball rose through the air like in slow motion. Time seemed to slow down. Danny wanted the moment to last for ever. Behind the goal stood his dad, smiling.

The goalie saved the penalty. And of course it was still raining. But somehow it didn't matter any more.

Barrington Stoke would like to thank all its readers for commenting on the manuscript before publication and in particular:

Rebecca Balaam
Daniel Girting
Dawn Groach
Aidan Hill
Philip Hillas
Charlie Inge
Catherine Jenkins
Jacqueline Johnson
Kate Mills
Natalie Piovesana
Leslie Robson
Abigail Thornton
Lauren Elizabeth Trask
Clare Twiselton
Paige Williams

Become a Consultant!

Would you like to give us feedback on our titles before they are published? Contact us at the email address below – we'd love to hear from you!

info@barringtonstoke.co.uk
www.barringtonstoke.co.uk

Great reads – no problem!

Barrington Stoke books are:

Great stories – from thrillers to comedy to horror, and all by the best writers around!

No hassle – fast reads with no boring bits, and a story that doesn't let go of you till the last page.

Short – the perfect size for a fast, fun read.

We use our own font and paper to make it easier to read our books. And we ask teenagers like you, who want a no-hassle read, to check every book before it's published.

That way, we know for sure that every Barrington Stoke book is a great read for everyone.

Check out www.barringtonstoke.co.uk for more info about Barrington Stoke and our books!

Guilty?
by
Eric Brown

A dead body.
Blood on the knife.
Nicky's fingerprints are
everywhere.
But is he guilty?
You can be the judge.

Two Words
by
Tanya Landman

Two friends.
A hiking trip.
A mistake that changes
everything.

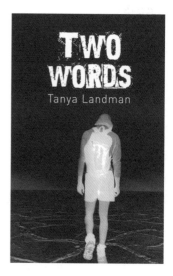

You can order these books directly from our website at
www.barringtonstoke.co.uk

Don't Call Us
by
Pat Thomson

The gang want Jack to help them steal some games consoles.
They will get him if he says no.
What can he do?

Mind-Set
by
Joanna Kenrick

Mark and Shaleem are best mates.
But the bombs change everything.
Will Mark stand up for Shaleem when it matters?

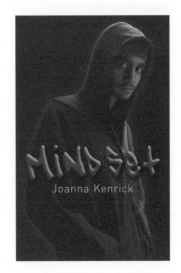

You can order these books directly from our website at
www.barringtonstoke.co.uk